Mermaid Mysteries

Sula

and the

Singing Shell

First published in Great Britain in 2012
by Boxer Books Limited.
www.boxerbooks.com

Library of Congress Cataloging-in-Publication Data

Kit, Katy.
Sula and the singing shell / by Katy Kit ; illustrated by Tom Knight.
p. cm.—(Mermaid mysteries ; 3)
Summary: Coral, Melody, Jasmine, and Rosa are trapped during a bad storm and if
Sula is to rescue her friends, she must find a magical shell with the power to calm the sea.
ISBN 978-0-8075-5090-8 (hardcover)—ISBN 978-0-8075-5091-5 (pbk.)
[1. Courage--Fiction. 2. Mermaids—Fiction. 3. Magic—Fiction. 4.
Princesses—Fiction.] I. Knight, Tom, ill. II. Title.
PZ7.K67119Su 2012
[Fic]—dc23
2011034167

ISBN: 978-0-8075-5090-8 (hardcover)
ISBN: 978-0-8075-5091-5 (paperback)

10 9 8 7 6 5 4 3 2 1 LB 15 14 13 12

For more information about Albert Whitman & Company,
visit our web site at www.albertwhitman.com.

Mermaid Mysteries

Sula

and the

Singing Shell

Katy Kit

Illustrated by Tom Knight

Albert Whitman & Company
Chicago, Illinois

Contents

CHAPTER 1

Ghostly Voices

Sula was waiting alone outside the Merschool for her mermaid friends to arrive. The Merschool choir had been invited to King Neptune's Palace to sing in a concert to honor Princess Rowena, who was visiting from the

South Sea. There was to be one last rehearsal before the performance the following afternoon. Sula shivered in the cold winter water and looked nervously around.

"Sula . . . Sula . . ." a ghostly voice called.

Sula peered into the gloom, but there was no one around. She must have been hearing things. *Where are they?* she thought impatiently. *They're not usually late.*

"Sula . . . Sula . . ." the ghostly voice called again.

This time, Sula started to feel

frightened. Her eyes grew large, her heart beat fast, and soon, every scale on her tail was standing on end. How she wished her friends were here.

Suddenly, out of the murky water, in a flash of shimmering color, something appeared.

"Aaaaaaaahh!" Sula screamed.

"It's only me!" cried Jasmine gleefully.

"Oh my goodness," said Sula. "I thought you were a ghost. I almost leaped out of my scales!"

Just then Rosa, Melody, and Coral swam up. "Sula, what's the matter?" asked Rosa. "What happened, Jasmine?"

"I was only teasing," said Jasmine mischievously. "But Sula's such a frighty fish. I'm sorry, Sula."

"I've got a lively imagination, that's

all," replied Sula, feeling a little foolish.

The friends went quiet.

"And a beautiful voice, too," said Coral, trying to cheer Sula up. "No wonder Madam Octavia chose you to sing the solo."

"Come on, let's go in. Everyone will be waiting for us," said Melody.

"Yes," said Rosa. "Madam Octavia wants our song to be note-perfect tomorrow. It's not often we have a real princess visiting Mermaid Bay, after all!"

The mermaids followed Rosa
along a path lit up by tiny starfish that
led to the school door. They talked as
they swam.

"I can hardly wait to meet the
princess," said Sula, brightening up.

"It's going to be really exciting. Tell us some more about her, Coral. You've seen her before, haven't you? What does she look like?"

"Well, she's tall and graceful," replied Coral, "with a beautiful silver tail and long, dark hair. But the most wonderful thing about Princess Rowena is that she is incredibly kind."

"Kind!" sneered Muriel, one

15

of the older mermaids in the choir
who was following them in. "More
like a busybody. Ever since that huge
storm in the South Sea that destroyed

the merfolks' homes, all I've heard about is her offer to help. It's 'Princess Rowena did this, Princess Rowena did that.' I mean, please!"

"I agree," said Myrtle, her twin sister, joining in. "What exactly can a royal princess do? She has no idea what they're going through. They don't need her help. I'm sure they can manage on their own."

"Muriel! Myrtle! I can't believe what you're saying. You're lucky it didn't happen to us," said Rosa, pushing open the rehearsal cavern door.

"Come in, come in, my darlings,"

boomed Madam Octavia, the
mermaids' music teacher. "How are we
all feeling about our little performance
tomorrow? You will not let me down,
will you, my sweet things? King
Neptune does not often make such a

request. You must make him proud."

"Don't worry, Madam Octavia," said Rosa. "The performance will be perfect. None of us could bear to disappoint the king."

"Yes, he is special to us all, isn't he? And Sula, my darling, how is that voice of yours? Such a voice I have not heard in my whole life—and that is longer than any of you can possibly imagine," she chuckled.

"It's not good, I'm afraid," said Sula. "Just the thought of singing in front of an audience makes me feel terrible. I'm afraid that I will open my mouth tomorrow and nothing will come out."

"Don't worry, my darling," said Madam Octavia. "It's just your nerves. I will help you with some breathing exercises that will calm you down. You must look after your voice. It should be treated like a jewel and treasured so that tomorrow, and

forever, it will shine."

Sula smiled weakly, but she was really very worried. What if she let them all down?

CHAPTER 2

King Neptune's Palace

The following afternoon, the
Merschool choir swam out to King
Neptune's Palace. As the mermaids
drew close, they could see its familiar
outline clearly in the distance—an
elaborate collection of coral towers

surrounding a glittering crystal dome. Many of the younger mermaids hadn't been there before, and they chattered excitedly. The older mermaids were in high spirits, too, twisting and turning somersaults as they swam. Only Sula was quiet.

At the entrance, Madam Octavia gathered them all together.

"So how are you feeling, my darlings? Do you have the butterfly fish flitting around in your tummies?" she asked, her eyes twinkling with excitement.

"It's very grand," said Sula. "And just look at all those merfolk."

Merfolk throughout the kingdom had been invited to welcome the princess and listen to the choir. Sula's head was spinning with the thought of singing her solo in front of such a large crowd.

"You will be fine, Sula," said Madam Octavia encouragingly. "Once you're up on the stage, nothing will stop you from enjoying yourself."

But Sula was not so sure. And as the mermaids swam through the palace gates, the waters became busier and busier. Palace courtiers were directing the crowds to the concert hall, and the mermaids followed. Once inside, they could hardly believe their eyes. Soft, pearly light flooded in through the vast crystal dome, lighting up a stunning mosaic floor. At the front was a large stage on which the choir was to perform.

An hour later, the choir took its position in front of a packed concert room. Everyone was eagerly waiting to catch their first glimpse of the princess and to find out what song the choir would sing.

Suddenly, the hall fell silent. Everyone looked toward the door, and a chorus of ten sea horns announced the arrival of King Neptune.

"My fellow merfolk," King Neptune

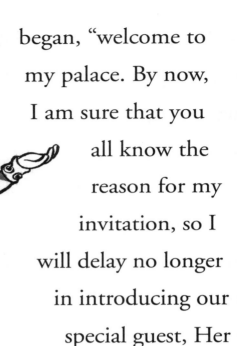

began, "welcome to my palace. By now, I am sure that you all know the reason for my invitation, so I will delay no longer in introducing our special guest, Her Royal Highness, the Princess Rowena."

And as King Neptune moved aside, the audience gasped. Behind him was the grandest-looking mermaid they had ever seen. She was wearing a floor-length golden coat woven from

26

the finest sea silk, and on her head sat
a dainty crown, studded with
a multitude of shimmering
precious jewels.

"Good afternoon, everyone, and thank you for welcoming me here to Mermaid Bay. Unfortunately, the reason for my visit is not a happy one," she began. "As many of you know, there was a storm earlier this year in the South Sea—a storm so terrible it destroyed almost all of the underwater homes in my kingdom, leaving many of the merfolk nowhere to live. The merfolk are rebuilding, but it is slow work. If everyone could donate just one item, small or large," she appealed, "something that can be used in the new homes—it will make

a huge difference to their lives, and
I will be eternally grateful."

The crowd clapped, and everyone
pledged their help. Only Sula was
silent. She was so
nervous about
singing, she had
barely heard a
word. Now
her mouth
felt dry and
her head felt
dizzy. How she
wished she could swim down from the
stage and join the audience instead.

Then, suddenly, she heard King Neptune's voice.

"And now, please sit back, relax, and listen to some of the finest voices we have here in Mermaid Bay. The Merschool choir, under the direction of Madam Octavia, will perform

'Guardians of the Sea.'"

As the choir sang the first line of the song, Sula's heart sank. She couldn't even remember the first line of her solo, let alone sing it. Fixing her eyes on Princess Rowena's kind face for inspiration, she tried to breathe slowly,

just as Madam Octavia had taught her. It worked; her nerves melted away, and Sula sang her solo louder and clearer than ever before. King Neptune smiled proudly throughout, and at the end, the audience clapped and clapped.

After the concert, Princess Rowena swam over to congratulate the mermaids. She asked Sula and some of the others what their names were and grasped each of their hands warmly as they replied.

"It really was the most incredible singing I have ever heard," she said.

"Is Madam Octavia your teacher? She tutored me years ago when I was a young mermaid, but we soon had to give up the idea of me ever being able to sing. Isn't that so, Madam?"

"Yours is a rare voice, Your Highness.

We just couldn't find the right song, that all," the music teacher replied tactfully.

"We both know that is simply not the case," said the princess. "We tried hundreds." Then, turning back to the mermaids, she continued. "Sula, on the other hand, could sing anything beautifully, I am sure. In fact, have you seen King Neptune's collection of singing shells? I am sure you would find them interesting."

Princess Rowena led Sula out of the concert hall and into a small cavern. Rosa, Melody, Jasmine, and Coral, not wanting to be left out, followed behind.

The cavern was lined with shelves
full of interesting objects. There were
mother-of-pearl combs, old silver
mirrors, gemstone necklaces, boxes of
all shapes and sizes, and, at the end of
the room, there were two rows of the

most beautiful conch shells they had
ever seen.

"Are these the singing shells?" asked
Jasmine.

"Yes, that's right," replied Princess
Rowena. "They belonged to mermaids
from long ago. Many of the songs

have been passed on, and we still sing
them today, but for others, these are
the last records."

Sula picked up a smooth pink shell.

"Would you like to listen to it?"
Princess Rowena asked her. "Most of
the shells are hundreds of years old,

and the songs are fading. But if we sprinkle them with magic sand, they still sing."

"Oh yes, please," said Sula.

Princess Rowena took some magic sand from her purse and sprinkled it over the shell. Gradually, the mermaids heard the voice of an unknown mermaid singing.

"It's magical," Sula whispered.

"Well, some of them really *are* magical," said the princess. "Look at this blue shell, for instance. It's full of songs that can change the seasons: a song for summer; another for winter. This green shell holds a song that can put a shark in a trance; and if you listen to the purple shell, you will hear a song that helps mermaids swim as fast as dolphins."

The mermaids spent a few more minutes looking at the singing shells. They really were stunning. Then, just as they were about to leave, Jasmine noticed something.

"What's this gap here for? It looks like one is missing." she said.

"It is," replied Melody, "I read about it in the Merschool library a few months ago. There was once a singing shell that held two songs that were used by mermaids to control the seas. One song whipped up a storm, and the other calmed it down."

Princess Rowena looked thoughtful. "I could do with that shell today," she said. "When I think of all the homes that were destroyed in the South Sea storm . . . If I had that singing shell, I could make sure it never happens again. Could you show me the book, Melody? We may be able to find out where the shell went missing. Perhaps then we could look for it."

"I'd love to," said Melody excitedly.

"Good," replied Princess Rowena. "I'll be at the Merschool at nine-thirty tomorrow morning. Don't be late!"

CHAPTER 3

The Lost Shell

The following day, Melody met Princess Rowena at the Merschool gates. "Just follow the coral," she said, leading the princess along a path lined with brightly colored sea fans. "The library is just this way."

Melody pushed open a shell-studded door. Inside was a circular cavern. It was lined from floor to ceiling with rocky shelves, which were laden with books. Jasmine, Rosa, Coral, and Sula were floating around a large, flat rock in the center, waiting for them. Myrtle and Muriel were there, too, pouring over a book of spells.

"This is where I read about it," said Melody, pulling a large book down from one of the shelves. "*The Chronicles of Mermaid Bay* by Iona Friel." She placed it on the rock for everyone to see.

The book was very old. Its seaweed-woven cover was tattered around the edges, and inside, some of the pages were torn.

"Thank goodness for waterproof octopus ink," she said, turning its pages. "The writing is still very clear."

"Look, here it is: *The Legend of the Singing Shell*," Jasmine exclaimed.

Then Melody began to read. "Thirty years ago, a great storm broke out in Mermaid Bay. It was no natural storm. Instead, it was started by a

magic singing shell. During the storm,
pirates who were passing through
Mermaid Bay managed to steal the
singing shell from the mermaids and
hang it on the ship's mast."

"I'm sure you all know the stories
of how cruelly pirates used to treat
mermaids," said the princess. "They

often tried to capture them and take them ashore."

"That's just it," said Melody. "It's thought that the mermaids used the singing shell to whip up a storm and avoid being captured. Once it was stolen, however, they were powerless to calm the waters down. The storm raged, the ship was wrecked, and all the pirates and many of the mermaids died. The shell went down with the ship and has never been recovered."

"How sad," said Sula.

"Look," said Melody suddenly. "There's a picture of a pale blue scroll drawn in the margin here. That means there should be a scroll containing a map somewhere—one that shows the position of the wreck."

She rummaged around in a chest at the foot of the rock. "Here it is," she announced, pulling out a tattered-looking scroll. The mermaids gathered around.

"Look! There's Crystal Grotto
and Splash Lagoon; that's Rainbow
Falls, and here are the Underwater
Gardens," said Coral.

"And here's the wreck. How would
we get there from the Merschool?"
asked Rosa.

Melody traced her finger from the
Merschool through Watery Downs,
past Crystal Grotto and Coral Reef,

and through Five Fathom Forest.

"The wreck lies just outside Mermaid Bay," she said.

"We could take you there and try to find the shell for you, if you like," said Rosa.

"That's very sweet of you," said Princess Rowena, "however, I'd like to think about it for a while. When I told King Neptune about the book last night, he was very worried. He says the songs in that shell are particularly powerful and can be dangerous if they are not used properly. He said it's probably better if the shell stays lost.

That's why no one has ever looked for it before."

"Oh, what a shame," said Sula, sensing the princess's disappointment.

Just then, Myrtle and Muriel floated over. "Perhaps we'll go and look for it instead," said Muriel. "Whipping up a storm or two. Sounds like fun."

"Yes, a huge storm would add a bit of excitement to boring old Mermaid Bay," replied Myrtle.

Princess Rowena was outraged. "How dare you speak like that, knowing the devastation your fellow mermaids suffered in the South

Sea? You ought to be ashamed of yourselves. King Neptune is right. It could be dangerous. No one knows how to use the shell properly now."

"We're sorry, Your Highness," mumbled Myrtle, going red. The

younger mermaids glared at the two older mermaids. The twins' carelessness didn't show the pupils of Mermaid Bay Merschool in a very good light.

"I should get going," said Princess Rowena abruptly. "Thank you so much for showing me the book, Melody. Hopefully we'll have the opportunity to meet again before I leave." And with a swish of her elegant silver tail, Princess Rowena sped off, leaving a trail of bubbles behind her.

As soon as she had gone, Rosa turned to Myrtle and Muriel. "How insensitive of you to upset Princess

Rowena like that. No wonder she wanted to leave. We're supposed to be making her feel welcome," she said crossly.

But Myrtle and Muriel just ignored her and went back to looking at their books.

"Come on," Rosa said to the others. "Let's leave these two alone. They obviously don't need friends."

CHAPTER 4

Rocky Ride

With little to do now that the
performance was over, the mermaids
decided to swim out to Rocky Ride.
Rocky Ride was one of the mermaids'
favorite places to play. Its towers of
rock were hollow, creating natural

water chutes. The mermaids simply climbed in at the top, waited for a wave to carry them down, and were ejected in a cascade of bubbles at the bottom. It was the perfect way to spend an afternoon.

They were almost there when a huge swell in the water carried them forward at high speed. The mermaids felt themselves being swept backward and tossed from side to side.

"Whatever is happening?" said Melody.

"I feel seasick," said Jasmine. "Oh, I wish it would stop."

The mermaids tried to battle on, but they were getting nowhere. Then, all of a sudden, the waters calmed down.

"We must have swum into a whirlpool," said Jasmine. "Oh well,

not far to go now. Race you there. First one to reach Rocky Ride's a princess."

The five mermaids finned furiously, though none more so than Sula, who got there first.

"Wow, Sula, that was fast!" said Rosa, who usually won all the races. "What got you going?"

"I'd love to be a princess," said Sula shyly. "Princess Rowena is so graceful and kind. I wish I could be like her."

"Well, here's your chance. You can be the princess today," said Melody. "You can start by choosing who's going to keep watch first."

One of the rules of swimming at Rocky Ride was that someone had to keep watch while all the others played. The chutes narrowed at the bottom, and often, the mermaids needed help to get out.

"I'll wait first," said Sula. "I think that's exactly what Princess Rowena would do."

"Well, how kind of you, Your Highness," said Jasmine with a bow. The others laughed.

"Come on, let's go!" shouted Rosa. Quickly, they shot to the surface

of the water, leaving Sula alone on
the seabed. As they reached the top,

the water started surging again, and
when they climbed into the chutes,
an enormous wave swept over them,
forcing them down, down, down—
faster than ever before.

Meanwhile, on the seabed, plants and sand were swirling wildly around. Sula could hardly swim.

Then, rocks started falling from the tops of the chutes. Sula noticed they were piling up at the bottom, trapping her friends inside. She fought her way over to them.

"Melody, Rosa, Coral, Jasmine!" she shouted. "Are you OK?"

One by one, the replies came back.

"A little bruised," replied Melody.

"My head hurts," murmured Rosa.

"My tail's trapped," called Coral.

"Help!" called Jasmine. "I'm scared."

"Don't worry," said Sula. "I'll move some of these rocks so you can wriggle out." She picked up some of the smaller rocks, but the larger ones were too heavy.

"I can't do this on my own," she shouted. "I'm not strong enough."

Suddenly, there was another huge

surge in the water, and Sula was thrown down onto the seabed. All around her, rocks were tumbling. Then she heard a scream.

"Sula, Sula, please!" pleaded Melody's voice from behind the rocks. "If this goes on much longer, the chutes may collapse. Quickly, Sula. Do something!"

CHAPTER 5

The Storm Makers

Sula lifted herself up from the seabed.

"Don't worry, I'll find some help," she called out to her friends. "I won't be long."

What am I going to do? she thought. Then she had an idea. Myrtle and

Muriel—surely they would help. Sula battled her way back toward the Merschool.

By the time she got there, the storm was so fierce that the school bell was ringing loudly. Sula hastily swam to the library, but there was no sign of the twins. *This storm is getting worse,* she thought. *Unless the sea calms down soon, the chutes may collapse.* Sula couldn't bear to think about what would happen to her friends. *If only I had the lost singing shell, I could calm the waters down,* she thought. *I know King Neptune has advised against it, but this is an emergency. I need it.* But to find it, Sula would have to confront her worst fear and swim through Five Fathom Forest and out to the wreck alone.

So Sula bravely set off. When she reached Five Fathom Forest, a tall wall of seagrass swayed wildly in front of

her. Sula took a deep breath, closed
her eyes, and swam on in. The water
was rougher here. It pushed and
pulled the long strands, which seemed
to grasp at Sula's tail as she passed.
Sula couldn't help
imagining
that all
kinds of
frightening
fish and
slimy sea
snakes were
following her. She was terrified. Only
the thought of her friends and the

danger they were in spurred her on.

After a while, the grass started to thin out, and when she opened her eyes, she found she was in a clearing. An old ship's bell stood rusting on the seabed in front of her. Sand was swirling madly around, making it difficult to see anything. She swam

over to take a closer look. Slowly, very slowly, a large, suckered tentacle curled around her tail . . .

"Aghhhh!" Sula screamed and darted off back into the seagrass, this time toward thick fans of sea bracken. Suddenly, a huge surge of water threw her forward. Tumbling head over tail, she lost her sense of direction. Now which way should she go? She wove her way around some thick stems of seaweed, and then she noticed a light in the distance. Could this be the end of the forest?

Soon, Sula was able to swim freely, and there in front of her was a faint outline of the wreck. *At least the map was right,* she thought. Silently, Sula

swam toward it. The sea was at its
roughest here, and water surged back
and forth through the ship's broken
bow. *I wonder if there are ghosts,*
she thought. Sula moved up toward
the deck. Suddenly, a hand grabbed
her shoulder . . .

She froze, too frightened even
to scream.

"What are you doing here?" said
a familiar voice.

"Princess Rowena!" Sula exclaimed.
"I thought you went back to
the palace."

"Yes, but on the way this huge storm broke out, and I realized that despite King Neptune's warning, someone must have come out here to find the

singing shell after all. I must say, I'm pretty disappointed in you, Sula."

"Me?" said Sula in astonishment.

"You think it was me who caused
this storm?"

Just at that moment, Sula and the
princess heard a noise.

"Help, help! Is anyone there?"
came a faint voice from behind
the mainmast.

Sula and the princess swam over.

Myrtle and Muriel lay on the deck,
the ends of their tails caught beneath
a large beam of wood.

"What in the sea are you two doing
here?" asked Sula.

"We just wanted a bit of fun," said
Myrtle sheepishly. "We found the

singing shell tied to the mast just like
Melody said and used it to magic up
a storm."

"It was fun for a while. Then it
became much fiercer than we ever
imagined," said Muriel.

"The wreck started to rock in the

water, and a huge beam fell on our tails, trapping us here," continued Myrtle. "I dropped the shell—it's down there on the seabed—but we can't reach it to calm the sea down."

"Well, you've caused a terrible storm in Mermaid Bay. There's been a rock fallout at Rocky Ride, and the others are in danger," replied Sula. "I came here to find the singing shell to calm the waters down."

Quickly, Sula and the princess swam down to the seabed and picked up the shell. It was beautifully decorated with intricate carvings of mermaids on the outside. Taking some magic sand from her purse, Princess Rowena sprinkled it over the shell. The two mermaids waited.

"Storm or calm?" floated out a mermaid's voice.

"Calm," said Sula firmly into the mouth of the shell.

Instantly, one of the sweetest voices they had ever heard filled the stormy waters. The mermaids were mesmerized as they listened to its words.

"Peace over water, peace over water.
Peace over water in the sea.
Peace over water, peace over water.
Peace over water in the sea."

As the song worked its magic, the notes from the beautiful voice were carried away, one by one, smoothing each surge of water before moving on to the next.

Soon all the water was calm and still, and the two mermaids swam back to the deck.

"Please can you free us?" said Myrtle. "It's really uncomfortable lying here trapped."

With the help of Princess Rowena, Sula lifted the heavy beam from the older mermaids' tails.

"Thank you," said Muriel meekly. "I'm sorry we were so rude to you earlier, Princess Rowena."

But Princess Rowena was in no mood to accept the apology. "This was not a smart thing to do," said Princess Rowena to the mermaids. "Not a smart thing to do at all. It sounds like

your fellow mermaids need some help.
Perhaps you can begin to make up for
some of the chaos you have caused by
returning to Mermaid Bay with Sula
and rescuing them. I'll return to the
palace to make sure the damage hasn't

been too great there."

"What about the singing shell?"
asked Sula.

"I think it's best if I give it to King
Neptune. He will keep it safe."

Sula handed Princess Rowena
the shell, and, as quickly as she had

appeared, Princess Rowena was gone.

"Come on," said Sula to Myrtle and Muriel. "Let's hurry. The others will be wondering where I've gone. Princess Rowena must wish she'd never shown us the singing shells in the first place. I wish you'd left it alone."

CHAPTER 6
Sula's Surprise

The following day, all the mermaids were recovering after their stormy adventure. Apart from a few scratches and bruises, they were all fine.

"Why in the sea did you do it, Muriel?" asked Rosa angrily. "We could have been seriously hurt."

"It just started out as a bit of fun," said Myrtle. "We didn't realize the storm would be so difficult to control."

"Well, thank goodness for Sula's bravery. Swimming through Five Fathom Forest alone is her greatest fear, you know," said Coral.

"I just can't believe you did it, Sula!" said Jasmine. "You, the scaredy-fish. Who would have thought you could be that courageous?"

"And now we've received another invite to King Neptune's Palace. I wonder what that's about," said Coral.

"He probably wants to tell us off. We went against his wishes—and Princess Rowena's. When she left me at the wreck, she was really upset," replied Sula.

"Well," said Rosa, feeling sorry for Sula, "She might understand. She is very kind."

So once again, the mermaids swam back out to the palace. This time, they were shown into the collections cavern to wait. Sula looked at the shelf containing the shells. The beautifully decorated singing shell was filling the space that had been empty just a few days before. King Neptune *did* have

a full collection now. Perhaps that meant he wouldn't be too angry.

As he entered the room, followed by Princess Rowena, Sula waited anxiously.

"You and your friends are most welcome, Sula," he said in a gentle but stern voice. "Princess Rowena has told me all about your bravery yesterday. How, soon after your fellow mermaids found the singing shell to add to my collection, they accidentally dropped it and released the storm song by mistake. Then she told me how you battled through the waves to help

your friends by using the singing shell
properly."

Sula looked astonished. Princess
Rowena, who was standing behind
the king, just smiled.

"Singing shells can be very

dangerous if placed in the wrong hands," he said, turning around to look at Myrtle and Muriel. "So I have invited you here today, Sula, to celebrate your courage. To show our gratitude, Princess Rowena and I have a gift for you."

Princess Rowena stepped forward and handed Sula a box. "Go on, open it," she urged.

Carefully, Sula opened the box. Everyone gasped. Inside was a pure white shell.

"It's your very own singing shell, Sula," said King Neptune. "With the help of a little magic sand, you can record a special song: a song that will be of use to you throughout your life and then passed on to help others."

"Thank you," said Sula. "What a wonderful gift. I shall have to choose my song wisely. There are so many I might need."

"That is certainly true," said King

Neptune, "but there is one song you will never need."

"What's that?" asked Sula.

"A song for courage. You have

shown us you have plenty of that already, Sula," replied King Neptune. And everyone agreed.

Here is a sneak preview of the next

Mermaid Mysteries
Book 4

The Spring Ball, missing gemstones,
and a backfiring spell.

There's a mystery to be solved—and the
young mermaid detectives are on the case!

CHAPTER 1

Dressing Up

"Ruby, sapphire, diamond, emerald, opal, pearl," said Melody, pointing one-by-one at the gemstones that were laid out on the seabed in front of her. The five mermaid friends had gathered out at Coral Reef to make clothes and jewelry for the Mermaid Bay Spring Ball. Surrounded by fields full of silky seaweed, dainty sea pods, sparkling sea stars, and golden seagrass, it was the perfect place to spend an afternoon.

"What about this one, Melody?" asked Rosa, picking up a clear blue stone and holding it up to the light.

"That's aquamarine," replied Melody, pushing her glasses back on her nose. "It's called that because it's the color of seawater. In Latin, *aqua* means water and *marine* is just another word for sea."

"Latin, what's that? You're so clever, Melody," said Rosa. "How do you know all these things? All I know is that it will make a wonderful necklace. Will you hold this strand of silver seaweed, please, so that I can tie it in place?"

Melody held the delicate strand while Rosa threaded the gemstone on. "There . . ." she said holding it up. "Perfect!"

All the mermaids were skilled at making jewelry, and they loved dressing up. The Spring Ball gave them the perfect excuse.

"Do you remember last year's ball?" said Jasmine. "Myrtle and Muriel were determined to arrive in style, so they persuaded a dolphin to pull their carriage. It swam at top speed and took a shortcut through Five Fathom Forest. When they arrived, Myrtle's top was torn to tatters and Muriel's tiara was bent out of shape. They thought everyone was laughing at them—they were furious for weeks."

J KIT   8/12

Kit, Katy.

Sula and the singing shell